The Secret Animal Society

RUTH SYMES would like to have a small dragon
for a pet (or even a well-behaved big one).
She lives in Bedfordshire and when she isn't
writing she can be found by the river walking her
dogs, Traffy and Bella (who are often in the river,
although they've never seen a sea serpent).
Find out more at: **www.ruthsymes.com**

The **Secret Animal Society** series

Cornflake the Dragon
Spike the Sea Serpent
Snowball the Baby Bigfoot

The **Bella Donna** series

Coven Road
Too Many Spells
Witchling
Cat Magic
Witch Camp
Bella Bewitched

THE SECRET ANIMAL SOCIETY

Snowball
The Baby Bigfoot

By Ruth Symes

Illustrated by Tina Macnaughton

Piccadilly
PRESS

First published in Great Britain in 2015 by Piccadilly Press
Northburgh House, 10 Northburgh Street, London EC1V 0AT

Text copyright © Ruth Symes 2015
Illustrations copyright © Tina Macnaughton 2015

A CIP catalogue record for this book is available from the British Library.

ISBN: 978-1-84812-463-9

1 3 5 7 9 10 8 6 4 2

Printed and bound by Clays Ltd, St Ives Plc

www.piccadillypress.co.uk

Piccadilly Press is part of the Bonnier Publishing Group
www.bonnierpublishing.com

For lovers of cornflake cakes and animals,
especially Esme, Jasmine, Evie, Mia,
Martin, Eric and Sharon xx

With thanks to Brenda Gardner,
SAS publisher and animal friend xx

A letter from the author ...

Dear Reader,

Thank you so much for looking inside this book. I really hope you enjoy reading about Cornflake the little pet dragon and the bigfoots. ☺

Cornflake's cornflake cakes in the book are very easy to make - you don't need to be a bigfoot to enjoy one!

You need:

50g of butter
3 tablespoonfuls of Golden Syrup
or runny honey
100g chocolate (any sort - even a
chocolate bar or a spare Easter egg
would do)
75g of cornflakes
paper cake cases

Gently melt the butter, Golden Syrup
or honey and the chocolate in a
saucepan (or pop it in a big bowl and
melt it in the microwave). Then stir
in the cornflakes. Spoon the mixture
into cake cases and put them in the

fridge to set. (If you don't have any cake cases handy you could spread the mixture on a plate and make one giant cornflake cake to cut into slices.)

Eat and enjoy! If you'd like to, you can add sprinkles or marshmallows to the mixture - just use your imagination.

If you do make some, we'd love to see a picture at the Secret Animal Society website - www.secretanimalsociety.com

PROLOGUE

The baby bigfoot stood at the entrance to the hidden cave and looked down at the twinkling festive lights in the valley far below. Behind him lay his mum and his dad and his two older brothers. They were all curled up together on

1

the bed of dried moss and pine needles they'd collected earlier in the year. His dad had his head tilted back and his mouth open as he snored. His mum made high whistling sounds as she breathed in and out. His older brothers were both fast asleep too and had been so for months. But now it had started to snow. It was time to wake up from the summer hibernation.

The baby bigfoot looked over at his family and blinked. A few moments ago he'd been lying in the middle of them, fast asleep as well. He looked back at the twinkling lights. They were so pretty.

His five-toed feet left little prints in the snow as he headed towards the sparkling lights. And the falling snow soon covered his tracks.

CHAPTER 1

It was never completely silent at the Secret Animal Society sanctuary. During the day you might hear the woolly mammoths calling to each other, the unicorns whinnying as they played in the long grass, the flying pigs squealing, the rainbow sheep baaing and the one hundred-and-one other sounds the secret animals that lived there made. It was almost as noisy at night when the nocturnal creatures came out. Laughing owls hooted as they flew amongst the trees, blue foxes barked, midnight goats bleated. Although the Tasmanian tigers were mostly quiet as they crept about, apart from the occasional yip.

Nine-year-old twins, Eddie and Izzie, and their three-year-old brother, Toby, had got so used to the sanctuary's night-time sounds that now they slept right through them. But their dragon, Cornflake, who shared Eddie and Toby's room, wasn't asleep.

He'd woken up when the snow started to fall. Now he was perched on the windowsill looking out at the whirling white flakes and making happy little cawing noises while Eddie and Toby slept on.

Last summer, Cornflake had been a school library lizard. When Eddie and Izzie had taken him home to the flat they used to live in, the children hadn't known he'd grow into a dragon. They still didn't know quite how old he was or how big he would grow but at the moment Cornflake was a bit bigger than Toby and a bit smaller than Eddie. About the size of a large dog.

There was just enough room for Cornflake and Toby to fit onto Toby's bed together, and so that's where the dragon usually slept. Sometimes Toby had his stuffed toys on the bed too and then it was a bit of a squeeze.

And sometimes, when he got too squashed, Cornflake liked to sleep in the toybox instead.

But tonight the dragon was too excited by the snow to sleep. He put out a claw to the glass to touch a snowflake that had landed on the other side of the window.

And that's when he heard it. Even though it sounded like it was coming from a long way away the sudden unexpected roar was still so loud it shook the window and made Cornflake jump. It was unlike any other animal sound he'd heard before. Cornflake trembled when a second roar followed the first one. He wasn't frightened, though. He trembled because he knew, as did the other animals at the sanctuary, that the roar was a secret animal's distress call. Something truly terrible had happened.

Cornflake hopped back onto Toby's bed and pulled the cover up over his head.

In the bedroom opposite her two brothers' room, Izzie was asleep too. Or at least she was until a thud of earth and pebbles landed on her window and woke her up. She hadn't had a room of her own when they'd lived in the flat. That was before their dad got the job of sanctuary caretaker and they came to live here, deep in the countryside.

Once she had a room of her own she'd decorated the lemon-coloured walls with drawings and posters of different animals. Everyone at the Secret Animal sanctuary loved animals, which was just as well, as there were a lot of them to love. Mostly the animals lived outside but sometimes, if one of them needed some extra care, they came to stay indoors for a while. Izzie

liked it when they did that.

She especially liked bottle-feeding the baby animals. She'd never even seen a lamb up close before they came to live at the sanctuary. But now she'd held a bottle for a tiny, thirsty lamb to drink from, and watched as it fell asleep in her arms. It hadn't been just an ordinary lamb, of course. It had come from the flock of rainbow-coloured sheep that lived on the hillside at the sanctuary. And once the lamb was strong enough it had gone back to its mum.

The first thud of earth on Izzie's window was quickly followed by a second, which was followed by a high, urgent, screech-like cry.

'Huh?' she said, sitting up in bed and rubbing her eyes.

The second thud was followed by a third thud and now there was more screeching, and it sounded like maybe there was more than one *something* out there.

Izzie slipped out of bed, pulled back the curtain a crack, and peeped out. There was a full moon and flakes of snow danced in the night wind.

She looked down at the snow-covered ground. Dad had built Doris the dodo a straw-filled snug chicken house, with an extra large door, so she'd be nice and warm in the winter. Doris's house was just below Izzie's window but she couldn't see Doris and she was sure the big bird wouldn't have thrown the earth and pebbles and she certainly wasn't making the screeching. Doris was much too shy and polite for that sort of behaviour. Izzie could barely even see Doris's house because of the falling snow. But she could just make out something else moving about down there. Something white.

Thuds of earth and pebbles also landed on Eddie, Toby and Cornflake's bedroom window. Cornflake made worried groaning sounds from Toby's bed. Eddie's eyes flashed open and he sat up fast, immediately wide awake.

'What's going on?' he said.

'Not get up yet,' moaned Toby, and he slung his arm round Cornflake's neck as if the dragon were a teddy bear.

Eddie jumped out of bed and headed over to the window to look out. Cornflake made a grumbling sound as he crawled out from under the covers of Toby's bed and came to join him.

'It's snowing,' Eddie said with excitement. He'd been wishing and wishing that it would snow and now his wish had finally come true. There was snow everywhere on the ground and in the trees, and it was still falling heavily. Eddie grinned, his nose pressed to the glass.

But then a clump of earth hit the window right where he'd pressed his face to it. Eddie quickly ducked back and waited a few seconds before he looked out again, trying to see who – or what – had thrown it. It was hard to make out anything clearly because of all the falling snow.

Cornflake made a worried *caw* sound beside him and tapped at the glass with one of his sharp claws.

Eddie squinted through the snow to where Cornflake was pointing.

'It looks like . . . almost like . . . but it can't be, can it?' Eddie said to Cornflake. But the dragon couldn't talk and just shrugged instead. 'They can't move,' Eddie said to himself.

'What is it?' Toby asked, rubbing at his eyes but not getting out of bed.

'Snowmen!' Eddie said.

He ran across the room and threw open the door just as his twin, Izzie, ran across her room and threw open her door and the two of then bumped into each other on the landing.

'Walking snowmen!' said Eddie.

'Polar bears!' said Izzie.

CHAPTER 2

At that moment there was a thumping on the front door followed by the high screeching noise again and, in the distance, a worryingly loud roar. Cornflake flapped his leathery wings and flew down the stairs.

Eddie and Izzie ran after the dragon as Toby clamboured out of bed.

'Wait for me!'

Eddie and Izzie had only just reached the middle stair when their dad, the new caretaker of the sanctuary, opened the front door. Noah, the retired sanctuary caretaker, was right behind him.

Outside stood two strange creatures. They weren't the walking snowmen Eddie thought he'd seen or the polar bears that Izzie thought she'd spotted.

These creatures were white like snowmen and furry like polar bears. But snowmen don't usually make screeching noises and polar bears, as far as Izzie knew, didn't knock on doors or throw clumps of earth and pebbles at windows.

Izzie thought the faces of the two animals
that stood at the door were a bit like the
faces of orangutans, with sharp intelligent
brown eyes. Their arms were much longer
than her own but they stood on two legs the
same as people.

Eddie looked down at the creatures' feet. Even though thick white fur covered most of their bodies, their five-toed feet were bare and furless. He bet their toes were cold. His were and he was indoors.

'Hello,' Dad said. 'Can I help you?'

The two creatures, who were a bit bigger than Eddie and a little smaller than Dad, started to make urgent grunting and growling sounds. They screeched again and waved their arms about.

'Bigfoots!' Noah said, his brow wrinkling even more than usual as he tried to understand what they were trying to tell them. 'Slow down now.'

'The falling snow must have woken them from their hibernation,' said Dad.

Eddie and Izzie looked at each other and then carried on down the stairs to the door. They'd learned about communicating with sign language at school, maybe it would help.

'What is it?' Eddie signed to the creatures by holding out his palms and tilting his head to one side.

One of the creatures pointed to Toby behind them on the stairs and then himself and then at Toby again.

'Me?' said Toby. 'Want me?' He pointed to himself and looked worried.

'Small?' guessed Dad, holding his hands a short distance width apart.

The two creatures nodded very fast and held up their thumbs. Yes. Then they made a cradle of their arms and began to rock them as if they were holding a baby and then they pointed at Toby.

'Baby?' said Izzie.

'I'm not a baby!' Toby told her. 'I'm three.'

But Izzie was right. There were lots more nods and thumbs up again. Then the two creatures pointed into the distance and help their paws up to their eyes.

'Something's very wrong,' Noah said. 'I've never known bigfoots to come to the door before. They're very shy creatures.'

'Looking . . .' Izzie said, trying to work out what the bigfoots wanted to tell them.

'Far . . .' said Eddie.

More nods but they still weren't quite right. They pointed to Toby and then made

the baby rocking movement again and then
pointed into the distance again.

'Baby . . . far?'

'Looking . . . baby . . .'

'Lost!' said Izzie.

The two creatures jumped up and down
with excitement and then pointed at
everyone and then out into the night and
made beckoning gestures.

'They want us to help them,' said Eddie.

'To find the baby,' said Izzie.

Dad was already pulling his coat on over
his pyjamas and stuffing his bare feet into
his winter boots.

'Of course we'll help,' he said.

'We'll get dressed,' said Izzie, turning to
run up the stairs.

'Me too,' said Toby.

But Mum didn't think that was a good idea.

'Not you, Toby,' she said. 'And not you, Eddie, or you either, Izzie.'

'But Mum!'

'It's not fair!'

'I'm sorry, loves. I know you'd like to help, of course you would, but it's just too dangerous out there at night in the snow. Plus you have to go to school later.'

Eddie and Izzie knew how very important it was that the sanctuary remained a secret. Alfonzo, the head of the Secret Animal Society, had explained that the easiest way not to draw any attention to it was for them to act like ordinary children – which meant they went to school every day. They hadn't been at the school nearest to the sanctuary for very long, but they'd both been chosen to star in the school's Christmas show. Eddie was playing the part of Santa Claus and Izzie was one of his helpful elves.

The last day of term was later on this morning and in the afternoon everyone was coming to see the show.

'You have to be at school in the morning,' Mum said. 'You can't let them down.'

'An hour,' begged Izzie.

'Just let us look for an hour and then we'll go to bed,' Eddie said.

'We promise,' Izzie added, when she saw that Mum was wavering.

'Young eyes are sharp,' Noah said softly.

'Not a minute more than an hour,' Mum told Eddie and Izzie, looking sternly at Dad and Noah as the twins raced to their rooms to get dressed.

'Me too,' said Toby hopefully.

But Mum shook her head as she pulled down her own coat. 'Definitely not you.'

Noah's wife, Beth, came to the top of the stairs in her long nightdress and slippers, yawning.

'What's going on?' she asked, as she pulled the earplugs she always wore at night out of her ears. She said she had to use them because Noah snored.

'A baby bigfoot's lost,' said Toby.

'Would you mind keeping an eye on

Toby?' Mum asked Beth. 'I need to help with the search.'

'Of course not,' Beth said, as she came down the stairs. 'But what . . . how?' She saw the two bigfoots standing outside the front door. 'Oh my goodness . . .'

'I tell you all 'bout it,' said Toby, taking hold of Beth's hand.

By the door, Cornflake had his head tilted to one side as he looked up at the slightly taller of the two bigfoots.

'Caw!'

But the bigfoots were much more interested in Noah than the dragon. Noah had a beard and the two bigfoots cooed and made clicking sounds deep in their throats as they pointed at it.

One of them reached out to touch Noah's beard and then the other one did too.

'All right, all right, that's enough now,' Noah said, brushing their paws away.

Eddie grinned as he came downstairs and saw what was going on.

'Cornflake stay too,' Toby said, as Izzie ran down the stairs wearing the warm clothes she'd thrown on over her pyjamas.

But Cornflake didn't want to stay behind with Toby. He flew out into the snow with

Eddie and Izzie, the grown-ups and the two bigfoots. Beth closed the door behind them.

'Not fair,' said Toby.

'Time you were back in bed,' said Beth. 'You don't want to fall asleep at playschool tomorrow.'

'I'm not sleepy,' Toby told her.

'Well, you will be if you stay up all night.'

'Thirsty,' said Toby.

'How about some hot chocolate?' Beth asked him. 'That'll quench your thirst and help you sleep.'

'With strawberry cream?' asked Toby. Strawberries were his favourite food.

'Good idea,' Beth said, and they headed into the kitchen.

CHAPTER 3

Izzie shivered inside her coat as she followed the others out into the cold night air. At least the snow was falling less heavily now and the moon and stars were very bright. But it was still bitterly cold. She could see the warm breath coming from the bigfoots' mouths, just like she could see it coming from her own mouth and from Eddie's.

Cornflake gave a *caw,* flapped his wings and flew up and away into the night sky. The bigfoots pointed up at him and flapped their arms too. Then they put their heads together and made worried noises.

'He won't hurt the baby even if he does find him,' Izzie told them. She mimed stroking Cornflake, and she made cooing noises and smiled.

'He only really likes eating cornflakes,' Eddie said, even though he knew the bigfoots wouldn't know what cornflakes were and probably couldn't understand him.

'He'll help us find your baby brother,' Izzie

said. She pointed up at Cornflake, who she could soon only just see in the distance. She smiled and held up her thumbs and nodded. The bigfoots slowly nodded back, held up their thumbs too, and bared their teeth in what wasn't quite a smile, but nearly was.

Izzie looked at Eddie. She was a bit worried, really. They'd certainly try to find the baby bigfoot. But the sanctuary stretched for miles and miles and the poor little thing could be anywhere. There were no security cameras because of the very real risk of them being hacked into by a nosy parker. The last thing anyone wanted was for the location of the sanctuary to be discovered.

'We did try putting cameras on trees to

take automatic timed photos once,' Noah had told them when he'd first shown them around. 'Still got some of the pictures that got took.' And he'd pulled out his wallet and showed them some very close-up snapshots of animal's eyes and mouths and teeth, as the sanctuary animals investigated the cameras and accidentally took photos of themselves. 'None of the cameras lasted more than a day before they were broken,' Noah added, shaking his head. 'Some of the animals thought they were food. Didn't feel right taking pictures of them, anyway. This is their home. Why should the animals have to be filmed in it?'

33

It might have come in helpful to have those cameras now though, Izzie thought to herself. They might have been able to find the baby bigfoot much more quickly if the sanctuary had cameras.

'We'll split up into search parties,' Dad said, as he led them to the lighthouse next to the caretaker's cottage for supplies.

Eddie waited outside with Mum and the bigfoots while Dad and Noah went into the lighthouse with Izzie to get the walkie-talkies and strong torches they'd need.

While they were gone Eddie pointed to the two bigfoots and then to his own eye. Next he put his hand over his eye and pretended to be looking all around and then he pointed to the bigfoots again and held out his hands palms up to show he was asking 'Where did you look?'

The bigfoots pointed to the left, towards the woods, and made screeching sounds and shook their heads and put their paws up to their eyes. The woods at the sanctuary were vast.

'Here you go, Eddie,' Dad said, coming out of the lighthouse. He handed Eddie a torch.

Eddie pressed the switch to check it was working and the effect on the bigfoots when the torch came on was instant. One of them screeched and shielded his eyes with his paws and the other one dived into a forward roll and hid behind a dustbin.

Eddie quickly turned the torch off again.
But they were going to need to use them in
their search.

'It's OK,' he told the frightened bigfoot
beside him and the bigfoot lowered his paws.

'Come out now,' Izzie said, beckoning to the
other one who'd hidden behind the dustbin.

It came slowly back over to them but not

as close as before. Both bigfoots kept looking warily at the torch in Eddie's hand and making worried *coo* noises.

Dad decided the bigfoots didn't need torches.

'They can probably see better than us anyway,' he said. 'You go with Noah in the buggy, Eddie. Mum, Izzie and I will head out with the bigfoots on foot.'

'The bigfoots will be even more frightened of the buggy lights,' Eddie said. They were very bright.

'You're right,' Dad told him. 'Don't turn on the buggy lights until we've gone.'

At that moment there was an almighty roar in the distance that went right through them all.

Back at the caretaker's cottage, even Toby and Beth could hear the roar from inside with the door shut. It was so loud, Beth almost dropped the large glass vase of winter flowers and sprigs of berries she'd just re-filled with water. Toby fell back onto the seat of the armchair he had been standing on to peer out of the window. Luckily he'd finished his hot chocolate with strawberry cream because the empty mug landed upside down on the carpet.

'Wh-what was that?' he asked, as the roar came again. The noise went up and down like a wolf's howl. But it definitely wasn't a wolf.

'I think it's the bigfoots' dad calling out,' Beth said.

'Why's it all woo-oo-ey?' Toby asked.

'So it can be heard a long way,' Beth told him.

'Wants to find baby,' Toby said, and Beth nodded.

The roar was even louder outside. Eddie couldn't understand what the two bigfoots were saying but he could see they were very worried when they heard it. One of them pointed towards where the roar had come from and made chattering sounds as if it wanted to go. But the other shook his head and pointed at Dad, and then the ground where he was standing, as if he wanted to stay.

The howling roar came again, and this time it sounded closer, and definitely angrier.

The first bigfoot pulled at the second one who'd wanted to stay. He pointed in the direction the roar had come from and gave a high screech.

'It's OK,' Izzie said. They reminded her of Eddie and her when their parents were calling them and they didn't want to get in trouble.

The next moment the two bigfoots ran off towards the sound of the roar and were gone.

'Right, let's go and find this little lost bigfoot,' said Eddie.

He and Noah went to the barn to fetch the buggy. Izzie, Mum and Dad headed off along a narrow grass track in the opposite direction. Finding a baby bigfoot wasn't going to be easy. But maybe it was frightened and wanted to be found and would come to them.

Izzie switched on her torch and shone it from left to right. She heard the crack of twigs as disturbed animals ran away from the bright light.

'This way,' said Dad, and they headed to the left.

CHAPTER 4

Eddie opened the double barn doors wide as Noah pulled the waterproof sheet off the three-wheeled buggy they used to give out the animal food around the sanctuary.

'They were smaller than I imagined bigfoots

would be,' Eddie said, as Noah started it up.

'That's because the two we met weren't fully grown,' Noah told him. 'Once they're adults they'll be a lot bigger than your father and me, and a lot stronger too. There's a good reason sanctuary caretakers are told to never wake a sleeping yeti!'

'So are yetis the same as bigfoots?' Eddie asked him. 'And abominable snowmen and sasquatches are they all the same too?'

'Pretty much as far as I can see,' said Noah, as he drove out of the barn. 'There's orang pendeks, almas, yeren, wendigos, yowies and snømannen too, you know. All seem to be pretty much alike.'

'People have found yeti footprints,' Eddie said. 'I read about it in a book.'

'Yes, there's been sightings all right,' Noah said. 'And usually the sightings are when the bigfoots are just coming out of their summer hibernation and not properly awake yet. They sleep from April till December each year.' He pushed his foot down on the pedal to speed up. 'We need to get that baby back to its parents as soon as possible.' He steered the buggy towards the beach.

'You don't think it's gone in the sea, do you?' Eddie asked him.

'I hope not,' said Noah. 'But we need to check the beach just in case.'

'Can bigfoots swim?' Eddie asked.

But Noah only shook his head. 'I don't know.'

'What do they eat?'

'All kinds of vegetation. They're perfectly

suited to living out in the wilds so long as no one disturbs them.'

There was lots of driftwood on the beach and Noah slowed down so Eddie had time to shine his torch at any possible hiding place.

'There!' Eddie said, when he saw a pair of eyes shining in the torch beam. But as they got closer they saw the eyes were much too big for a baby bigfoot. It was Spike the sea serpent. His son, Serpy, was sleeping curled up with his mother. Spike gave a low growl in greeting.

But they didn't have time to stop.

Noah drove on with the bright buggy lights shining. Once they'd checked the beach they headed on up along the track into the hills. From the top of one of them Eddie looked down at the town in the valley below where he and Izzie went to school. It was full of twinkling lights and looked very pretty.

'Oh no,' he said.

'What is it?' Noah asked him.

'You don't think he's gone down there, do you?'

'I hope not,' Noah said grimly.

They both knew that if the little bigfoot was seen it could cause a media sensation. When Spike had been trying to bring baby Serpy back home to the Secret Animal

Society sanctuary and he'd been spotted out at sea there'd been TV crews everywhere out looking for him. Hunters too.

'If it's caught . . .' Eddie started to say.

'The poor little thing will probably end up in a cage at the zoo for people to stare at,' Noah finished.

Izzie, Mum and Dad were over by the waterfall.

'It's been more than an hour,' Mum said, looking at her watch. 'Time we were heading back.'

Izzie didn't want to go home without finding the lost baby bigfoot. But there hadn't been so much as a glimpse of him. They'd heard the terrifying roar-howl from the adult bigfoot every now and again. It didn't sound as if the baby had been found. It still sounded desperate and angry.

They'd only seen Cornflake once. He'd been flying across the sky ahead of them, his strong leathery wings flapping.

It had taken the dragon a long time to learn how to fly. A long time, and a lot of jumping off chairs at the flat where they used to live, but once he'd got the hang of it there was no stopping him. Izzie wondered what he could see from up there.

Beside Noah in the buggy, Eddie tried really hard not to yawn but as it grew later and later he couldn't help it. Noah steered the buggy back to the cottage. Eddie's head was nodding by the time they got there and he woke up with a jolt when they stopped at the front door.

'Go on now. In you go. Get some rest,' Noah told him.

'But ...'

'You can help again tomorrow.'

Eddie didn't want to go inside but he didn't have much choice. He'd promised he'd only be out for an hour and it was already almost two.

The cottage door was never locked and he let himself in.

Toby was fast asleep on the sofa with Beth asleep beside him. Eddie didn't want to wake them so he crept past and went up the stairs. His Santa Claus costume was hanging from a hook on the wall. Tomorrow was the big show day. They'd been practising for it for weeks and he'd been really looking forward to it. But now he wished he could be outside in the cold tomorrow looking for the lost baby bigfoot instead.

When he got to his room, Cornflake hadn't come back yet. But Eddie wasn't too worried. The little dragon sometimes went off to play with the big dragons and could be gone overnight. Cornflake was free to go wherever he liked for as long as he liked now they were living at the sanctuary, unlike when Eddie had first met him. Then the poor little thing had lived in a small tank on the library windowsill and looked like a sickly grumpy lizard. Eddie sometimes thought that he and Izzie had only just found the baby dragon in time. It wasn't until they'd let Cornflake out of the tank that he'd started to grow. In a few short weeks he'd grown wings and learnt to fly. The first time Cornflake had flown off by himself he and Izzie had been terrified he wouldn't come back and imagined him lying injured somewhere. But fortunately that hadn't happened. Alfonzo, the head of the Secret Animal Society, had found him and brought him back to the flat. Without Cornflake they'd never even have known that the Secret Animal Society existed and Dad wouldn't have got the caretaker job here at the sanctuary.

Eddie looked out of his bedroom window. He could see the torches of Izzie, Mum and Dad as they headed back to the cottage.

'I'm too worried about the baby bigfoot to sleep,' Izzie said, as Mum and Dad left her at the door, telling her to go up to bed.

'Just try,' Mum told her.

'We'll keep on looking,' Dad said, and the two of them headed back along a different track as Izzie watched them go. She really wanted to be out there still helping. If only there was something else they could do.

'Any luck?' Eddie asked her, poking his head out of his door as she came up the stairs.

Izzie shook her head and went into her room. Eddie's room looked out of the front of the house but Izzie's was at the back, looking towards the lighthouse. As she stared out of the window she realised there was one thing they hadn't tried.

'Quick!' she said to Eddie, opening his door, and she and Eddie left the cottage and ran to the lighthouse. They pulled open the door and headed up the steps. There were two hundred and sixty-nine steps in total and the light-room at the top had windows and telescopes all around it. The first few times they'd climbed up the stairs they'd been exhausted but they were a bit more used to it now and it was worth it.

They could see the whole of the sanctuary from the top of the lighthouse. Izzie knew it still was going to be almost impossible to spot a baby bigfoot in the darkness against the white snow, especially if it had fallen asleep and wasn't moving. But they had to try.

When they got to the room at the top Eddie pressed his eye to the first of the telescopes. In daylight he could have seen all the way to the black mountains but not at night. In the dark, even with a full moon, he couldn't see far. The snow was falling less heavily now but even the few flakes that there were made it harder.

'Anything?' Izzie asked a few minutes

later. She was looking through the telescope that was pointed towards the waterfall at the centre of the sanctuary – not that she could see it in the dark.

'No,' sighed Eddie.

They looked through all six of the telescopes. Looked and looked and looked. But they couldn't see a baby bigfoot anywhere.

Izzie rubbed her eyes.

There . . . did something move? No . . . maybe . . . just a bird. Or a dragon.

'See anything?' Eddie asked, from another telescope.

Izzie shook her head. 'Not really.'

Finally they gave up and went back down the stairs.

'Mum and Dad and Noah might have more luck,' Izzie said.

They shivered as they went out into the freezing night air.

'It might even be home already,' Izzie said. 'I haven't heard the adult bigfoot roar for ages.'

'I hope so,' said Eddie. He hoped so more than anything.

They trudged back through the snow to the cottage and finally went to bed.

CHAPTER 5

Every morning, whatever the weather, Eddie and Izzie helped to put out food for the sanctuary animals. They didn't all need feeding. The big dragons that Cornflake sometimes played with certainly didn't. But then they rarely saw those dragons unless they were coming to find Cornflake.

They'd never seen the bigfoots before last night either. But Noah had said they'd been hibernating throughout the warm months and they didn't need help finding enough food because they lived on vegetation.

Some of the animals, like Cornflake, had lived very unnatural lives before they came to live at the sanctuary. Some of them had never had to fend for themselves and didn't know how, or couldn't find their own food for one reason or another, and so the food was put out for them. The singing chickens had come from a battery farm where they'd never been out of their cages, seen the sun, or found their own food before they were

rescued and brought to the sanctuary

Doris the dodo always came running over to Izzie to see if she had something tasty for her. Doris loved all fruit, but her particular favourite was peach. She ran round and round squawking with delight on the rare occasions Izzie had one of those for her.

Izzie didn't have a peach for Doris this morning but she did have some sliced apple.

Doris pecked the cut up slices from Izzie's hand with her funny-shaped beak.

'Hope those bigfoots didn't frighten you last night,' Izzie said.

Doris made a lot

of squawking noises that sounded to Izzie that maybe they *had* frightened her. But she still ate the rest of the apple slices, so she was obviously OK now.

Once Doris had finished eating Izzie went to help Eddie feed the other animals.

The unicorns mostly ate grass but still liked the food Izzie and Eddie brought for them as well. The unicorns were hard to spot, as they were shy, but in the winter they put hay and carrots in the unicorn barn for them and it was usually all gone by the next morning. All of the animals were free to go wherever they liked in the sanctuary. But not all of them liked being out in the cold and it wasn't always easy to find food, especially for the grass-grazing animals when the ground was covered with snow. That's why there were dry animal shelters scattered around the sanctuary so the animals could get away from the cold and the rain when they wanted to.

Normal sheep would have been hard to spot in the snow but luckily it was easy to see the rainbow-coloured flock that lived at the sanctuary.

'It's lucky the sheep are so many different colours,' Eddie said, as they headed across the crunchy, icy grass. More falling snow in the early hours of the morning had covered up any footprints they might have found, but it had stopped snowing now. As they fed the animals Izzie and Eddie kept a look out for the baby bigfoot.

'Maybe it's found its way back home already,' Izzie said.

'I hope so,' said Eddie. But he couldn't help thinking that if the baby bigfoot was back home they'd have heard an almighty roar of joy from the baby's mum and dad.

The woolly mammoths were used to the cold with their thick coats to protect them. But they still came heading over to the children as soon as they saw Eddie with a wheelbarrow full of carrots and potatoes and Izzie with a wheelbarrow piled high with hay.

'One at a time now,' said Eddie, but the woolly mammoths didn't listen to him.

'Don't push,' Izzie laughed, as the mammoths trunks dived into the hay, covering her in stray bits as they did so.

The flying pigs came swooping down to their trough from the rafters of the pig house as Eddie and Izzie poured the buckets of vegetables and pig nuts into it. Some of the animals, like the flying reindeer, were migratory. 'Noah said they'll be flying away soon,' Eddie told Izzie, as they watched

the flying reindeers munching on the hay they'd brought for them. There were other sanctuaries all over the world for them to go to.

As Eddie was collecting more food from the food barn he bumped into something hard and metal. It was covered in sacking.

'Ouch!' he said, as he rubbed his elbow.

'What is it?' Izzie asked him.

Eddie pulled up a corner of the sacking and peered under it.

'Don't know but it's very red,' Eddie said.

Noah was always fixing up some piece of machinery or other. But this definitely wasn't a tractor or an engine.

Izzie peered under the sacking from the other side.

'It's got a bench seat and a handle,' she said.

'There's a harness and reins at the front,' said Eddie.

Eddie and Izzie often agreed on things, without needing to say a word. It was a twin thing. Now they were both silently agreed that they *had* to see what was under the sacking and so together they pulled it away. But what they discovered was a real surprise.

'A sleigh!'

'It's huge.'

Then they had the same thought.

'You don't think it's a Christmas present for us from Noah, do you?' Izzie said.

Eddie gulped, because that was exactly

65

what he was thinking. It was the only explanation.

'We can't let Noah know we've seen it,' Eddie said.

Izzie nodded. 'He'd be so disappointed.'

They quickly pulled the sacking back over the bright red sleigh with gold hand-rails and trimmings. Then Eddie and Izzie filled up their wheelbarrows again and they headed back out into the snow.

It really was very cold and the pond that the golden geese usually liked to swim in was covered with thick ice.

Not that the geese felt like going in the pond today. They were tucked up with the singing chickens in the warm fowl barn. Their tummies were soon full of the corn the children brought. Izzie filled a large bowl of fresh water on the ground for if they got thirsty. Eddie spread out some fresh straw.

'Did you check all the water feeders and buckets weren't icy?' Izzie asked, as they left the barn.

Eddie nodded. 'I broke the ice on all the frozen ones.'

Neither of them wanted any of the animals to be thirsty.

'Better be getting back,' Eddie said, as Izzie blew on her freezing fingers.

CHAPTER 6

Izzie had grown used to the feeling that there were more creatures watching them than those she could actually see. Many of the animals at the sanctuary were frightened of humans, and with good reason, because humans weren't always kind to them. But today it felt different and when she looked round she saw the two young bigfoots peering out at them from the trees.

Izzie waved and the two bigfoots waved back.

Eddie beckoned to them and before heading over the bigfoots looked at each other and then behind them, as if they weren't quite sure if they should come or not.

They looked in the empty wheelbarrows and sniffed. Then they rubbed their tummies.

'Are you hungry?' Izzie asked, rubbing her own tummy and pointing to her mouth.

The bigfoots nodded.

Eddie and Izzie weren't sure what bigfoots

liked to eat but there was lots of food at the cottage and Beth would probably know, so they took the two teenage bigfoots home with them.

When they got to the cottage Eddie opened the front door but the two bigfoots looked worried and didn't follow him in. The more nervous of the two shook his head very fast and backed away.

'It's OK,' Izzie said. And she stepped into the cottage and waved to them to come in after her.

The first bigfoot put one foot on the doorstep and sniffed at the smell of breakfast cooking that was coming from inside the house. Then he looked back at the other bigfoot and beckoned to him. The other bigfoot shook his head and showed his teeth but the first bigfoot beckoned some more and made cooing noises. The other one came slowly forward and took his brother's hand. His eyes darted everywhere as he looked warily all around himself as they went inside.

They both blinked at the Christmas tree lights and made cooing sounds.

The braver bigfoot had a tuft of thick hair on top of his head and must have been very thirsty. He picked up the big glass vase full of festive flowers and berries, pulled out the flowers, tipped up the vase and noisily glugged down the water.

'Oh no – that's not what you do!' Izzie cried.

'That can't taste nice at all,' said Eddie.

71

'Yucky,' said Toby, coming out of the kitchen.

Meanwhile the more nervous bigfoot ate the flowers and berries that had come out of the vase.

Once the flower water was drunk and the flowers and berries eaten the bigfoots headed over to the twinkling Christmas tree making '*mmmmm*' noises.

'Oh no!' cried Izzie.

'Stop!' cried Eddie.

'No eat it!' shouted Toby.

The bigfoots looked at Izzie and Eddie and made confused noises. They backed away nervously as Dad came in from the kitchen.

'What's going on?' Dad asked, with Mum right behind him.

'You're back!' Izzie cried.

'Did you find him?' Eddie asked. But even as he asked the question he had already guessed, by their faces, that they hadn't.

Mum shook her head.

'Poor little thing wandering around, lost and frightened, all night long,' Izzie said. The baby bigfoot must be hungry too.

'We just came back for some food and then we'll head out to look again,' Mum said.

'What about Cornflake?' Eddie asked. 'Is he with you?'

'No, Noah and he are still out there looking,' Dad said. 'We saw Cornflake once or twice and told him to come back.'

'But he wouldn't,' Mum said. 'You know what he's like.'

The children nodded. A flying dragon, who could have been alive for hundreds of years as far as any of them knew, did what he liked.

'Come and finish your porridge,' Mum said to Toby, and they went back into the kitchen with the bigfoots following them.

But Toby didn't want porridge for

breakfast, not even with a spoonful of treacle in the middle.

'Yucky,' he said.

So Mum made him one of his favourite strawberry jam sandwiches instead.

'You have to eat something,' she said, 'or you'll be hungry.'

Toby liked strawberry jam sandwiches a lot but he was tired from the night before and took ages to eat even a quarter of it.

Mum rolled her eyes. She was tired too.

'Toby, hurry up and . . .'

'It's OK,' Beth said quickly. 'We'll take it with us when I drive the children to school. Toby can eat it on the way.'

'How about some cereal?' Izzie said to the bigfoots, taking down a box and shaking out  two bowls for them. She was worried that hot porridge might burn their mouths.

The bigfoots didn't use spoons and they didn't wait for Izzie to pour milk on it. They just tipped the bowls up into their mouths and crunched the flaky cereal all up in a few seconds. They'd just finished their first bowlful and Izzie was shaking out some more for them when Cornflake arrived back with Noah.

'Brrr – cold out there!' Noah said rubbing his hands together. 'What's for breakfast?'

The dragon gave an angry *caw!* when he

saw the bigfoots were eating his favourite cornflakes. He was so angry that he breathed out fire and the two bigfoots dived under the kitchen table.

'Oh dear,' said Izzie when she realised she'd used cornflakes without thinking. They always had lots of packets of them in because they were the little dragon's favourite food. And now it looked like he didn't want the bigfoots to eat them too.

'It's OK, Cornflake,' Izzie said, quickly shaking some more cornflakes into a bowl. 'There's lots for you.'

Cornflake made a *hmmph* sort of noise. But he didn't breathe any more fire and he sat down on his chair at the table and started eating.

Izzie took a packet of shredded wheat from the cupboard instead.

'You can come out now,' she told the bigfoots.

But they didn't want to come out from under the breakfast table, not even the bravest bigfoot. Izzie gave them the packet of shredded wheat and they ate the whole lot and some of the cardboard packet while they were still under there.

CHAPTER 7

'You'd better get ready for school,' Mum said to the children when they'd finished their breakfast. 'You don't want to be late.'

The sanctuary was well-hidden, which meant the secret animals were as safe from prying eyes as they could be. But being so far off the main roads meant it was also a long drive to school.

Izzie, Eddie and Toby headed upstairs and the two bigfoots came out from under the table and followed right behind them, obviously afraid of being left alone.

'This is our room,' Toby said, flinging open the door to the bedroom he shared with Eddie and Cornflake. The two bigfoots followed the boys inside.

'This my bed,' Toby said, flopping down on it. 'S'all nice and bouncy.' He patted the bed beside him. 'See.'

The two bigfoots looked at each other and then they headed over to Toby's bed. The braver one sat down on it gingerly.

'See – nice?' Toby said.

The braver bigfoot beckoned to the less brave one. The less brave one made a little moaning sound as if he wasn't quite sure if it was a good idea. But he gave it a try. As he sat down it bounced up and down a little, and then he bounced up and down a little more and gave a sound that could only have been a laugh.

Toby laughed too and Eddie grinned.

'Let's jump!' Toby said, and the next moment he was standing on the bed and jumping up and down on it.

'Um, I don't think that's a good idea,' Eddie said, but it was too late. The two bigfoots were already copying Toby and jumping up and down on the bed with him.

'What's going on up there?' Dad shouted from downstairs and everyone stopped jumping and looked at each other.

'Ready?' Izzie asked, coming over from her own room.

The braver bigfoot pointed at Eddie and Izzie and then at his eye.

'You want us to look . . .'

The less brave bigfoot pointed out of the window and then made the baby rocking movement and pointed at Toby.

'Am not a baby,' Toby said, crossly. 'Am a big boy.'

'Later,' said Eddie. He couldn't think of a sign to explain it to them.

'We have to go to school now,' said Izzie.

The bigfoots looked confused.

Then there was a giant roar from outside.

'It's their dad,' Toby told Eddie. But Eddie already knew that.

The two bigfoots went running down the stairs and out of the front door, leaving the children alone.

'Are you sure you want to wear a bumblebee fancy dress costume today?' Mum said, as Toby came downstairs wearing one. 'What about that lovely snowman costume I got you? You looked so sweet in it.'

Izzie and Eddie's headteacher, Mrs Peters, had written to the parents to say if anyone wanted to come in a snowman costume it would be much appreciated.

'*If as many people as possible come in snowman costumes then the audience can be part of the village of Snowtown too . . .*' she'd written in her letter home.

'Bumblebee,' Toby said firmly.

Mum sighed. She was too tired to argue and they needed to get back outside and look for the missing baby bigfoot. 'OK,' she said.

'I'll take the snowman costume with us too,' Beth said, and she winked at mum. 'Just in case.'

Eddie and Izzie came down in their school uniforms with their costumes in bags. They weren't going to put them on until this afternoon. But everyone at Toby's playschool was getting dressed up for the whole of the last day.

'We probably won't make it to the show,' Mum told Eddie and Izzie.

'Sorry,' said Dad.

'Toby and I will be there though,' said Beth. 'Won't we, Toby?'

Toby nodded.

Izzie and Eddie tried not to be too disappointed that Mum and Dad weren't going to be there as well.

'We want you to find the little bigfoot,' Eddie said.

'I can't bear to think of the poor little thing out there lost and alone,' said Izzie as they put on their coats.

Beth handed Toby his strawberry jam sandwich when they got in the minibus. 'There you are.'

'Thanks. Bees like jam.'

He took one bite and then put the rest of it in his coat pocket for later as Beth drove off.

When they got to town Beth dropped Izzie and Eddie off first.

'See you later at the school show,' she said, as Toby waved goodbye from his car seat.

Toby's playschool was next door to Eddie and Izzie's school but not in the same building. It had a large garden for the children to play in and there were four freshly made snowmen in the middle. Three of them had hats and scarves on, carrots for noses and stones for eyes. But the fourth one didn't have a hat or a scarf or an orange carrot nose. It wasn't even standing up like the others and looked like it was asleep on the ground until it opened its mouth.

'Snowman yawned,' Toby said, from his car seat.

But Beth shook her head.

'Snowmen can't yawn,' she told him, as she unclipped him from his car seat. 'They don't have mouths.'

But Toby knew what he'd seen.

As soon as she'd lifted him out Toby ran
over to the snowmen. The snowman who'd
yawned was standing up now.

'Toby – come back!' Beth shouted, and
ran after him. She grabbed hold of his

hand and led him into the playschool. Toby looked behind him and beckoned to the little snowman to come with him. But the little snowman started chewing on a carrot that used to be one of the other snowman's noses instead.

'Now you be a good boy and I'll pick you up later to go and watch Izzie and Eddie's school show,' Beth said, as she helped Toby take off his coat and hang it on a peg. Lots of the other children were wearing snowman costumes. But Toby was the only one dressed as a bumblebee.

Once Beth had gone, and everyone had started playing, Toby put his coat back on and headed back outside.

'Hello,' he said to the little snowman.

The little snowman sniffed and Toby saw he was crying real tears that ran all the way down his face.

'It's OK,' Toby said. 'Don't cry.' He held out the half-eaten jam sandwich he'd put in his coat pocket for later.

The little snowman took it and ate it in one big gulp.

'You must be very hungry,' Toby said, his eyes wide. He'd always thought snowmen were icy-cold but this one was all warm and furry. He liked warm and furry ones better.

'My name's Toby,' Toby told him. 'What's your name?'

But the little snowman didn't say anything so Toby thought of a name for him.

'I'll call you . . . er . . . er . . . Snowball?'

90

The little snowman put his arms round Toby and hugged him and Toby hugged his new friend back.

When the bell rang Toby took hold of Snowball's strawberry-jam-sticky hand and the two of them went into playschool together.

CHAPTER 8

In Eddie and Izzie's classroom at school, all the other children were very excited about being in the show. And very excited about it being the last day of term and almost Christmas.

'We're going to my Gran's. We always go there.'

'My dad's taking us skiing.'

'Mum wants some winter sun.'

'What are you doing for the holiday, Eddie?' Joe asked Eddie.

Eddie gave Izzie a look.

'Oh, just staying home,' he told Joe.

'Nothing unusual,' Izzie said.

It was the truth. It wasn't unusual for Eddie and Izzie but most children didn't get to spend their days with dragons and woolly mammoths and unicorns and dodos. They couldn't tell the other children, not even Joe, about the Secret Animal Society sanctuary.

'No one would believe us if we told them we had bigfoots jumping on our beds this morning,' Eddie whispered to Izzie when Joe went to get the class register.

'Quieten down now,' Mrs Peters, the teacher, said. But no one did and the room got even noisier instead. 'QUIET!' Mrs Peters shouted and at last everyone stopped talking. 'I know you're all very excited about it being the last day of term and the show this afternoon. But this is still a school day and school is all about learning, so we need to do some of that too,' she told them.

'Aaaw, miss,' said a boy at the front. 'Can't we just play games today?'

Mrs Peters shook her head. 'This morning, in honour of our play this afternoon, we're going to learn about Father Christmas. Did you know that once upon a time he used to wear green clothes instead of a red suit?'

As Mrs Peters told them about the different stories of Father Christmas from around the world, Eddie and Izzie did their best to concentrate and not to yawn, because they'd been up so late the night before.

'Santa Claus – or Sintaklaas, as he's known in Holland – was a very kind and very shy man,' Mrs Peters said. 'He was so shy that when he wanted to give some money to a poor family he climbed up onto the roof and dropped a bag of coins down the chimney rather than knocking at the door. The bag of coins landed in the sock of a girl who'd been drying them in front of the fire and that's how the tradition of hanging up stockings started,' she told them.

Eddie looked at Izzie and they both had the same thought. The bigfoots would have probably tried to eat any socks if they'd found them hanging by the mantelpiece.

'We use pillow cases instead of socks at our house,' Joe told her. 'You can get more in them.'

'In Lapland Santa Claus is rumoured to be a bigfoot, or snømannen,' Mrs Peters said, and Eddie's eyes opened wide in surprise.

They opened even wider when Mrs Peters showed them pictures of Santa's sleigh. Eddie

looked over at Izzie. She nodded because she'd been thinking exactly the same thing as her twin.

The red sleigh in their barn was the spitting image of the one in Mrs Peters' book. But why did Noah have it?

After break it was time for one last rehearsal of the school show. Eddie's school Santa Claus sleigh was made from cardboard that they'd painted red. He couldn't sit in it because it was flat. Eddie and Izzie walked on the unpainted side of it, and poked their hands through the holes they'd made, so they could carry it along.

The sleigh did have reindeers to pull it though, or at least children dressed up in reindeer costumes. Sanjay's costume had a bright red nose because he was the one pretending to be Rudolph.

Izzie was Santa's elf and had to wear a

green jacket and skirt, with red and white stripy tights and green boots with pointed toes that curled backwards. They didn't hurt her feet but felt a bit funny to wear and weird to walk in. The rest of the children were dressed in snowman outfits.

The show was called 'Santa Claus and the Snow Kids' and it told the story of how the snow folks of Snowland helped Santa Claus when his sleigh crashed in Snowtown.

Eddie had to wear a red padded Father Christmas suit and hat with a curly white beard that was so long it came all the way down to his knees. He also had to wear stick-on white bushy eyebrows that he didn't like very much because when he pulled them off they left little bits of glue behind.

Izzie's favourite part of the whole show was when she and Eddie got to throw out sweets to the audience. They did it from behind the red cardboard sleigh and there was a big bucket full of sweets all ready. But Mrs Peters said they didn't need to practice that bit again before the show.

CHAPTER 9

At Toby's playschool the children were sitting on the floor in a circle as Jenny, the new student teacher who'd only started that week, offered round a tin of foil-wrapped Christmas star-shaped chocolates. Most of the children were dressed as snowmen, but as well as Toby the bumblebee there was also a mermaid, Red Riding Hood and a spaceman. Jenny didn't know all the children yet and it was very confusing when they were all in costume. But she did her best because the other teachers were busy helping with the show.

'Thank you, Jenny,' said Toby, as he took a chocolate.

'You're very welcome,' Jenny said. She offered the tin to the little snowman sitting next to Toby. The snowman made a growly sort of sound as he took two chocolates.

'His name's Snowball and he can't talk,' Toby told her, as he unwrapped his chocolate.

'But he can make signs.' Toby put his thumbs up to Snowball and Snowball put his thumbs up to him.

Jenny had learnt some sign language at college and she put her hand to her mouth in the thank you sign and the little snowman copied her. Jenny smiled as she moved on to offer the chocolate tin to the next child in the circle.

Snowball looked at Toby. He was making *mmm-mmmm* sounds as he ate his chocolate. Snowball looked down at the two chocolates he'd taken from the tin and then back at Toby. He took one of his chocolate stars and was about to pop it in his mouth, with the foil wrapper still on it, when Toby stopped him.

'No, no – you have to take the shiny bit off!' he told his new friend. 'Here, I'll do it for you.'

Snowball watched as Toby took the wrapper off and gave the chocolate back to him and then he put the whole thing in his mouth.

'*Mmmmm-mmmm-mmmm,*' said Snowball and Toby smiled.

'Who'd like to do some finger-painting?' Jenny asked, when she'd given out the chocolates.

Toby's hand immediately shot up and he put Snowball's hand up for him too.

Jenny smiled at Snowball and put her thumb up and Snowball put his thumb up too.

Toby had liked Jenny before but now she could do sign language he liked her even more.

He stood up and Snowball stood up too and they headed over to the paints.

Once they'd finished their paintings  they got to make chocolate cornflake cakes with Jenny. But when Snowball heard the sound of tambourines shaking and drums banging and wooden sticks clacking he wanted to join in with that instead. He tried to join in with the singing but could only make growling sounds rather than words.

Jenny had learnt the sign language for 'Rudolph the Red-nosed Reindeer' at college and she showed everyone how to sign the words. Snowball loved learning the signs, especially the one for the word 'reindeer' where he had to pretend his hands were antlers at the side of his head and waggle his fingers.

'Play it again,' Toby begged when the song was over, so Jenny did. Snowball and Toby laughed and laughed as they did their reindeer signs.

Beth came to pick Toby up from playschool at lunchtime.

'My friend Snowball,' Toby told Beth who'd been rushing around doing some last minute Christmas shopping. He gave Beth the box of cakes he and Snowball had made with Jenny.

'Hello, Snowball,' Beth said. 'That's a lovely snowman costume.' She turned back to Toby. 'Do you want to wear your snowman costume too for Eddie and Izzie's show? It's in my bag all ready for you if you do.'

But Toby shook his head.

'Bumblebee,' he said.

Beth helped Toby put on his coat as Snowball watched them.

Lots of the other children had brothers and sisters in the show at the big school next door too. Everyone was so excited and it was so busy and noisy and the children all looked so similar in their snowman outfits that no one noticed the little snowman following Toby and Beth down the path.

CHAPTER 10

After lunch Eddie and Izzie got changed into their costumes.

Eddie always stuck his bushy white Santa Claus eyebrows on before he put on his Santa beard and moustache. One time he'd done it the other way round and he'd ended up with the eyebrows stuck in the beard. When he'd managed to pull them off they'd stopped being sticky and kept falling off.

The children who were acting as the snowmen in the show all had the same costumes but some of them had aprons or caps or hats and scarves on as well. Everyone had a fake carrot nose and big buttons for eyes and orange peel mouths. They had their feet covered in fluffy white material sticking out of the bottom of their costumes. Eddie thought they looked a little bit like penguins with their tummies joining their feet without any legs or ankles on show in between.

Izzie was ready first and went to peep round the stage curtains. She wanted Mum and Dad to be in the audience because if they were it meant that the lost baby bigfoot had been found. Her heart skipped when she thought she saw Mum sitting right in the front row, next to Toby, who was still wearing his bumblebee costume and eating a cake. But her heart sank when she realised it wasn't Mum at all, it was Joe's mum talking to Toby. He was the only one dressed as a bumblebee but there were lots

of snowmen in the audience because of Mrs Peters' letter home.

Izzie spotted at least two snowbabies in the audience and lots of Toby's playschool friends were dressed as little snowmen, as well as some of the bigger children and parents. There weren't any snowdogs in the audience but Eddie's friend Joe was pretending to be a snowdog in the show. He even got to bark and howl along with some of the songs.

Izzie smiled as she watched one of Toby's little snowmen friends come to join him as the lights were turned off and the blackout blinds closed. The two of them looked so cute all yellow and white squashed together on the seat eating cakes.

'Snowball likes cakes,' Toby told Beth in a

loud voice that Izzie could hear from the stage.

Mrs Peters beckoned Izzie away from the curtains as the school band started to play. It was almost time for the show to begin.

Izzie saw that Toby's friend was still sitting next to him when the curtains opened for the first scene of the show. It was set in Snowtown and the snowmen and snowdog did a dance at the end of it.

Toby and Snowball clapped and clapped as everyone took a bow. Snowball really liked clapping. Sometimes he clapped even when there wasn't really anything to clap at and he always joined in with the howling whenever snowdog Joe howled. Izzie thought Toby's friend was really good at howling. Especially for a little kid. It sounded even more like a real howl than Joe's one.

'Ssh, Snowball,' Toby said.

Beth gave Toby's snowman friend another cake to keep him quiet.

'He certainly does like cakes,' she whispered to Toby.

'We made them at playschool,' Toby whispered back.

From behind the stage curtain Izzie still wished Mum and Dad could have been there to see how well the show was going. But she knew it was more important that they found the baby bigfoot and got him safely back to his own mum and dad. She remembered how terrible it had been when they'd lost Cornflake before they came to live at the Secret Animal Society sanctuary. She'd been so frightened and worried about the little dragon, who'd been the size of a kitten at the time, lost and all alone.

The music for 'Rudolph the Red-nosed Reindeer' started to play and Toby's little snowman friend was so excited he immediately jumped off his chair. Izzie watched Toby and his friend doing the signs to the song as she and the rest of the cast danced and twirled around. Toby and his friend looked so cute.

It was almost time for Izzie's favourite part of the show – throwing the sweets into the audience. She and Eddie stood behind the red-painted cardboard sleigh with a bucket of foil-wrapped Christmas sweets next to them. As the band played a new tune they threw handfuls of sweets out into the audience.

Snowball was very good at catching them but every now and again Izzie heard Toby shouting, 'Don't eat the paper!'

Beth laughed and laughed when some of the sweets landed on top of her head and Snowball picked those off and ate them too. She looked at him closely. His furry costume didn't look quite so snowy white now that there was lots of smeared chocolate down his front and bits of silver crinkly paper stuck to him.

As Eddie, Izzie and the rest of their class took their final bows there was an almighty roar.

'Is it part of the show?' one woman asked.

'Can't be – the show's over,' said someone else.

Up on stage, Izzie and Eddie looked at each other. They'd heard that roar before. They knew what it was.

'Bigfoot!' they said.

Down in the audience, the effect of the roar on Toby's friend was instant. He gave a cry that turned into a howl and then as Beth watched the little snowman jumped off the chair he'd been sharing with Toby and ran out of the hall.

CHAPTER 11

'Quick!' Eddie said. He dropped the red cardboard sleigh and jumped off the stage. Izzie jumped after him.

'Snowball, come back!' Toby shouted, as he ran out of the hall after the little bigfoot.

Beth grabbed her bags and Toby's snowman costume and ran too. 'Toby! Wait!' she cried.

Everyone was standing up and getting in each other's way now and it was very noisy because they were all talking at once. People wanted to find out what had made the loud roar.

There were snowmen everywhere blocking the aisles. Izzie tried to push past them. She could hardly believe it. Toby had found the baby bigfoot. It had been sitting in the audience with him all the time.

Snowball didn't run the way most children do. He put his hands on the ground to help him run along like an orangutan does and he was very, very fast. Plus he could climb really high and swing from the lights and the gym ropes hanging round the walls whenever people blocked his way.

'We have to stop him,' Izzie said to Eddie, but it wasn't easy with all the people there.

She could hear the little bigfoot making high screeching, crying sounds as he ran. He was obviously terrified but the school was so noisy, and everyone was so distracted, that no one else seemed to notice. There were so many children dressed as snowmen that it was hard to keep track of Snowball amongst them all.

Eddie and Izzie ran one way and Toby and Beth ran the other. They came out of the school hall and towards the exit to the school gates.

'Can you see him?' Eddie asked.

Izzie shook her head.

They'd lost him.

'I'll go this way . . .' Izzie said, and she ran to the right.

'And I'll go this way,' Eddie said, and he ran to the left.

'We'll go straight ahead,' Beth told Toby, and headed to the crossing to cross the road.

Izzie ran as fast as she could along the road to the right. Ahead of her was the zoological park and, in front of it, just turning in, was the little bigfoot.

'Stop! Wait!' Izzie yelled, but Snowball

didn't stop or wait. He saw Izzie running towards him and jumped over the turnstile and ran into the zoo.

'You can't come in without paying!' the ticket lady shouted after him. But the baby bigfoot didn't stop.

Izzie didn't know what to do. She was still

dressed in her elf costume and she didn't have any money but she *had* to go after him.

'He's my brother,' she told the grumpy-looking ticket lady. 'Can I go and get him?'

The ticket lady sniffed. 'I've already alerted security with the emergency buzzer,' she said.

Izzie gulped as two fierce looking security guards came running over. Ahead, Izzie could see Snowball up a tree, swinging from branch to branch until Izzie couldn't see him anymore.

'Which way did he go?' the guards asked the ticket lady and she pointed in the direction that the little bigfoot had run.

'He's my brother – I saw him head over there . . .' Izzie said, pointing in the opposite direction. The security guards would only frighten Snowball more by chasing after him.

'Our security guards are very good,' the ticket lady told Izzie. 'They'll have caught him in no time.'

'Please can I go in after him?' Izzie asked desperately.

But the lady just shook her head. 'Best if you stay here and wait for your parents,' she told her.

Eddie came running up.

'He's in there,' Izzie said, pointing at the zoo. She couldn't see Snowball now but the baby bigfoot was in there somewhere.

'Oh no,' said Eddie. The zoological park was the last place he wanted Snowball to be. What if they realised he was a bigfoot?

They'd never let him go. 'We have to do something,' he said.

'We need to get in,' Izzie said. 'The lady won't let me in after him and I don't have any money to pay.'

Eddie looked down at the Santa Claus outfit he was wearing. It didn't even have pockets.

'Me neither,' he sighed.

They'd have to find Beth.

'Come on,' Izzie said, and the two of them went running off to find Beth and Toby.

There were still lots of snowmen about, making their way home from the school show.

Izzie and Eddie spotted Joe and his family.

'Hey, Eddie,' said Joe.

'Have you seen my little brother?' Eddie asked him. 'He's dressed as a bumblebee.'

Joe hadn't but Joe's dad had.

'I saw a bumblebee back there, just past the postbox,' he told Eddie and Izzie.

'Thanks!' they said and the twins ran off before Joe's dad could finish telling them how well they'd done in the show.

'Beth! Toby!' they shouted when they spotted them.

Beth and Toby stopped.

'We've found him,' Izzie said.

'Oh, that's good,' said Beth. 'Where is he?'

'He's in the zoo,' Eddie said.

'That's bad,' said Toby.

Izzie nodded. 'I know. We have to get him out.'

By the time the four of them collected their coats from school – Beth insisted they'd catch their deaths of cold in just their costumes – and got back to the zoological park the first ticket lady had gone on her break and there was a new lady there.

'Can I help you?' she asked them.

'Four tickets, please,' said Beth, and as soon as she'd paid they hurried inside.

'Where is he?' Toby said.

'We'll find him,' Izzie told her little brother. But she couldn't see the baby bigfoot anywhere and the zoo was a big place.

CHAPTER 12

Eddie, Izzie, Beth and Toby looked all round the zoo, twice, but they couldn't see Snowball anywhere and they couldn't ask anyone if they'd seen him either. They couldn't risk saying anything without possibly causing a lot of trouble for all the other animals at the Secret Animal Society sanctuary.

'Excuse me, please,' a zookeeper said to Eddie as he went past with some bananas.

'Yum, bananas,' said Toby. It had been a long time since lunch.

'These are for our new white ape,' said the zookeeper. 'He's very rare and we don't know much about him yet but I've never met an ape that didn't like a banana.'

'Where is he?' asked Izzie.

'I can't tell you that, I'm afraid,' the zookeeper said. 'He's not being shown to the public yet. He's very new. I probably shouldn't have said anything . . . ' the zookeeper said, his voice trailing off as Toby burst into tears.

'What are you going to do to him?' Toby sobbed.

'Just see if he wants a banana,' the zookeeper told Toby kindly. 'We've never had a white ape here before. He's bound to draw in lots of crowds and the ape experts can't wait to examine him.'

'Oh no!' said Eddie.

'You can't do that,' Izzie said.

'Should be free,' sobbed Toby.

'We'll be very kind to him,' the zookeeper said, 'and give him lots of nice food to eat. Come on, I'll show you.' And even though he wasn't supposed to, because he felt sorry for Toby crying, the zookeeper took them to Snowball's new home.

Snowball was sitting with his back to

them in a small cage with his shoulders
slumped, looking utterly miserable.

'How about a nice banana?' the zookeeper
said to the baby bigfoot's back and he pushed
one through the bars.

But Snowball didn't even so much as look
round and the banana stayed where it had
fallen on the ground.

'Snowball!' Toby whispered.

At last the little bigfoot lifted up his head and looked round. When he saw Toby he jumped up and started screeching and tugging at the cage bars as he tried to get free. Izzie saw that the keys were hung on a hook close to the cage but too far away for Snowball to reach.

'Maybe it wasn't such a good idea to bring you to see him,' the zookeeper said. 'Come on now, I think you'd better leave.'

The zookeeper ushered Eddie, Izzie, Beth and Toby round the corner as Snowball screeched and screeched.

'No I don't want to leave him,' Toby cried, stretching his hand out to Snowball.

Beth picked Toby up and hugged him to

her. 'Come on now, it's going to be all right, hush.'

Izzie looked back to see the baby bigfoot stretching his hand out through the bars, begging to be set free.

'We have to do something,' said Eddie.

'We have to get him out of the zoo and back to his mum and dad,' Izzie said.

'Poor Snowball,' said Toby, and he wiped his teary eyes on his bumblebee costume sleeve.

As Izzie watched him she had a very good idea. A way that they could help Snowball. But it all depended on Toby.

'Do you still have Toby's snowman costume?' she asked Beth.

'Yes,' Beth said, and she pulled the little

white costume from her bag.

'Toby, Snowball needs your help. Let him have your bumblebee costume and you wear the snowman one,' Izzie said to her little brother.

'Don't like snowman costume! S'all scratchy,' Toby complained.

Izzie gave him a look.

'Snowball needs it,' she told him, and she explained her plan to the others.

'OK,' Toby said, so Beth helped him take off the bumblebee costume and put the snowman one on instead.

From round the corner, Izzie could hear the zookeeper trying to encourage Snowball to eat a banana.

'Go on, try it . . . just a little bit, for me.

I'm sure you'll like it. Look, I'll have a bite. *Mmmmmm*. Now you have a bite . . .'

'We need a distraction to get the zookeeper away,' Izzie said.

Eddie nodded. He knew what to do.

'Help! Help!' he shouted. 'HELP!'

The zookeeper came running to see what was wrong. Eddie grabbed hold of his arm.

'One of the tigers,' he cried. 'Over there. Must have got out.' And he pointed off into the distance.

As soon as the zookeeper had disappeared, Eddie headed for the exit and Izzie, Beth and Toby hurried round to the little bigfoot's cage. This time Toby put his finger to his mouth and said 'Sssh' before Snowball could cry out.

Snowball nodded. He didn't make a sound

but he stretched his arms out through the bars of the cage and looked very sad.

'Don't worry. We're going to get you out,' Izzie told him.

Beth took the keys off the hook on the wall and unlocked the cage. The little bigfoot was trembling with fear.

'He likes these,' Toby said, and he gave Izzie one of the sweets she and Eddie had thrown from the stage during the school show.

When Snowball saw the sweet he hopped out of the cage and while he was unwrapping it and eating it Izzie got him into Toby's bumblebee costume and took hold of his hand.

Beth lifted Toby into Snowball's cage and closed the door.

'Be brave,' she told him. 'It won't be for long and I'll be right here.'

'I don't like it,' Toby said and Snowball cried out and tried to pull the bars from the other side.

'It's OK,' Izzie told Snowball who kept screeching and holding his arms out to Toby.

'Wait till we're away and then start shouting,' she told Toby and Beth as she picked the little bigfoot up and ran.

CHAPTER 13

'Help, help! Someone's locked a little boy up in a cage by mistake!' Beth shouted.

'HEEEEEELLLLLPPP!' Toby yelled at the top of his voice from inside the cage.

The zoo security guards came running.

'What's going on?' they asked.

'This little boy shouldn't be in there,' Beth said, pointing at the cage.

Toby pulled off his snowman costume hood.

'We've been looking for a little boy who'd gone missing,' the first security guard said.

'Just went running through the zoo,' said the second.

'No sign of the parents anywhere.'

The first security guards quickly opened the cage door.

'You'd think the zoo would know what was a child and what wasn't,' said Beth, as Toby scrambled out of the cage.

As they hurried out of the zoo together she phoned Noah from her mobile phone and told him what had happened.

'We need help fast,' she said.

'I know just what to do,' Noah said, and he quickly told her his plan.

Izzie ran on through the zoo with Snowball in her arms. She could see Eddie waiting for them at the exit when a voice shouted: 'Stop!'

Izzie's heart sank but she didn't have a choice. She stopped and put Snowball down, dreading whatever was going to happen next.

A man holding a camera approached them. 'That's a fantastic bumblebee costume your little brother's got on,' he said. 'It'll show up really well amongst all the pictures of children dressed as snowmen I've taken for the newspaper today. Say cheese . . .'

And the photographer snapped a picture of Snowball in the bumblebee costume. Izzie saw two security guards run past them towards the cage that Toby was now in.

'Got to be going,' Izzie told him, and she took hold of Snowball's hand and hurried away.

Eddie was waiting for them outside the gate.

'You made it,' he said.

'Only just,' Izzie told him.

At that moment there was another loud bigfoot roar. Snowball cried out in reply.

'If his parents come into town and are spotted they'll bring prying eyes to the sanctuary,' Eddie said.

The twins knews that all the animals that had been safe and made their home there would be in grave danger.

'We can't let the secret of the sanctuary get out!' Izzie said, as they hurried down the street with Snowball.

'Eddie! Izzie!' a voice shouted. It sounded like Noah.

Eddie looked round but couldn't see him.

'Up here!'

Eddie looked up. Above them in the sky, Noah was in the sleigh that had been under the sacking in the barn. Not only that but Cornflake was flying in front of the sleigh, flapping his wings, as he guided two of the flying reindeer and four flying pigs.

'Just like Rudolph,' said Izzie.

'Almost,' said Eddie, as Snowball pointed upwards and cooed.

Unlike Rudolph, Cornflake was using

fire instead of a red nose to show the way through the falling snow.

Cornflake swooped down to them, and the sleigh landed. As soon as Eddie, Izzie and Snowball had got into the sleigh he took off again with the reindeers and flying pigs flapping their wings behind him.

It was time to take the lost baby bigfoot home.

'Use this,' Noah said, handing Eddie a handbell. 'And put your elf hat on, Izzie.'

Eddie rang the bell as Cornflake breathed out a giant flame of fire.

'Everyone will know about the sanctuary now,' Izzie said, as people on the ground pointed up at them.

But Noah shook his head. 'Some things are just too crazy to believe,' he chuckled. 'Like Santa Claus and his elf, together with a bumblebee, flying in a sleigh led by a fire-breathing dragon, reindeer and flying pigs.'

And Noah was right. The people on the ground were looking up at them but not quite believing what they saw.

'What is it?'

'Is that Rudolph?'

'Looks more like a dragon to me.'

'Those can't really be flying pigs . . . can they?'

'And why's there a bumblebee in the sleigh?'

'I heard it's for a new film,' Beth told everyone they met, including the TV press, as she and Toby came out of the zoo, just as Noah had told her to do. 'A big publicity stunt.'

Cornflake guided the flying reindeers and pigs all the way back through the snow to the bigfoots in the woods.

When they looked up at the sleigh and saw Snowball they knew it was him, even though he looked like a bumblebee, and gave a huge cry of joy. Snowball cried back. Noah didn't even have time to land the sleigh before Snowball jumped out and ran to them.

The bigfoots were so happy they hugged and hugged him to them and made growly sounds.

'Time for us to go home too,' Noah said, and Cornflake flew back to the cottage with all the flying pigs and reindeers, Noah, Eddie, Izzie and the sleigh behind him.

CHAPTER 14

As soon as the sleigh landed Eddie and Izzie released the reindeers and pigs from the harness. Eddie fetched fresh water for them to drink and Izzie gave them lots of tasty carrots to say thank you for all their help.

'I don't know what we'd have done without you,' she said.

Cornflake heard her and made a *hmmph* sort of noise.

'You helped us more than anyone,' Eddie told the dragon. 'How about making some cornflake cakes to celebrate?'

Cornflake always thought that cornflake cakes, or anything made from cornflakes, was a very good idea indeed.

'I'd better get this sleigh polished up spick and span,' said Noah.

In the cottage kitchen Cornflake munched on a few flakes as he watched Eddie stir the melted chocolate, golden syrup and butter into a large bowl of cornflakes. Then he watched as Eddie carefully spooned the mixture into ten little cake cups in the muffin tray.

But the dragon didn't like it when Eddie put the tray of cakes in the fridge and coughed a little flame of fire in protest.

'They'll be much nicer if we let them set,' Eddie told him.

'*Hmmph*,' said Cornflake.

He sat next to the fridge to make sure no one else ate the cornflake cakes when he wasn't looking.

By the time Toby and Beth arrived back in the minibus, the cakes were ready.

Eddie took them out of the fridge and Cornflake pointed at Toby who was still wearing his snowman costume.

'You want him to have one?' Eddie asked,

while Beth tried to get in touch with their Mum or Dad on the walkie-talkie to let them know that the baby bigfoot had been found.

'Hello? Hello?'

Cornflake nodded so Toby had one cake and Cornflake had nine.

'I can't get hold of them,' Beth said after a few moments. 'It's all crackly. I'll see if Noah's been able to get hold of them.' And she headed out to the barn.

Once the cakes were gone Eddie and Cornflake made some more. Eddie had one, Izzie had one, Toby had one and Cornflake had seven and then they made some more.

'That's a lot of cornflake cakes!' Izzie said.

'Cornflake go pop!' said Toby.

Eddie thought so too. But Cornflake *had*

saved the day by leading the flying pigs and reindeers and Santa's sleigh through the snowy sky. If Cornflake wanted cornflake cakes – lots and lots of cornflake cakes – then he could have them. But this had better be the last batch. Beth and Noah would be back soon.

'I see you decided to wear your snowman costume after all,' Mum said to Toby when she and Dad came in with Beth. 'I knew it was a good idea to take it with you.'

'That's not why I'm wearing it,' Toby told her. 'I'm wearing it because a baby bigfoot's wearing my bee clothes.'

They'd all only just finished telling Mum and Dad the whole story when there was a loud thump on the door. Dad opened it to find the whole bigfoot family standing outside.

'Snowball!' Toby shouted when he saw his friend. He beckoned the bigfoot family inside.

'Um, I don't think that's a good idea,' Mum started to say. The adult bigfoots were twice the size of the two young ones and three times the size of Snowball. But it was too late. The bigfoot family were already walking through the front door.

The bigfoot dad was so tall he had to bend his head and crouch down a little just to get in. Eddie held his breath as the massive

creature stopped and sniffed his hair. He didn't want to be bigfoot dinner. But then the bigfoot dad made a soft growly noise and gave Eddie a friendly pat.

Snowball ran to Toby and hugged him and Toby hugged him back.

The mother bigfoot gave Izzie a twig.

'Th-thank you,' Izzie said.

Then the bigfoot mum gave bits of twig to Mum, Dad, Eddie and Beth too. She pointed at the thin twig and then to Izzie's mouth.

'You want me to eat it?' Izzie asked. She wasn't at all sure about eating a twig.

'It's OK,' Beth told her as she put the twig to her own mouth. 'It's liquorice root. We grow it here and the unicorns love it. It's what's used to make liquorice sweets.'

Eddie chewed his twig. It did taste of liquorice.

'I like it,' Izzie decided, as she tried it too. She smiled and held her thumb up to the bigfoot mum. The bigfoot mum held up her own thumb and showed her teeth.

The braver of the two younger bigfoots had a reed basket full of wild nuts and seeds that he gave to Mum. The less brave one had a huge bouquet of winter flowers and holly branches. It was so big he was almost hidden behind it.

'Oh, that is nice,' Beth said, as he gave the bouquet to her.

Cornflake came out from the kitchen and made a cawing sound to Eddie.

Eddie quickly went back into the kitchen

and took Cornflake's cakes out of the fridge.

'Cornflake would like you each to have one,' he said, as he offered round the tray. Everyone took one and made *mmmm-mmmmm* noises.

Cornflake ate the rest.

'Come on, Snowball,' Toby said, when the little bigfoot had finished his cake. He took hold of Snowball's sticky chocolatey hand and the two of them headed up to Toby, Eddie and Cornflake's room.

'This is my bed,' Toby told the little bigfoot, as he climbed on to it and stood up. 'It's all nice and bouncy.'

They were bouncing up and down on Toby's bed. Christmas music started to play downstairs. When Snowball heard 'Rudolph the Red-nosed Reindeer' he gave a screech and bounded downstairs with Toby right behind him. The baby bigfoot started to do the signs that he'd learned at playschool with Toby.

'Play it again, Dad. Play it again,' Toby said, when the song was over.

And Dad did play it again – and again – and again until everyone knew all the signs and were joining in. The older bigfoots turned out to be just as fond of music as Snowball was. They made growly noises as they sang and signed and use improvised instruments to join in with the other Christmas tunes that were now playing.

Cornflake started dancing along to the music and the bigfoots joined in with that too.

But then the less brave bigfoot accidentally stepped on the television remote and the TV screen came on. None of the bigfoots had ever seen a television before. The bigfoot mum dived behind the sofa, the bigfoot dad hid behind the curtains, the brave bigfoot curled up in a ball on the carpet and the less brave bigfoot jumped so high in alarm that he ended up swinging from the light on the ceiling.

'It's OK,' Izzie said, and she held up her thumbs. 'Nothing to be scared of.' And she went over to the TV and touched the screen.

The mum and dad bigfoot crept out from behind the sofa, and the curtains. The brave bigfoot uncurled himself and the less brave one let go of the light and dropped to the floor. They looked behind the TV and then scratched their heads. But then Dad put 'Rudolph the Red-nosed Reindeer' back on again and everyone soon forgot about the TV.

It was very late and the moon and stars were shining brightly by the time the bigfoot family finally left.

'Do you think they'll come back to see us again?' Izzie asked Dad. But Dad didn't know.

'I hope so,' said Eddie.

And everyone else hoped so too.

CHAPTER 15

The next morning Eddie, Izzie, Dad, Mum and Noah headed out to feed the sanctuary animals, just like they did every morning.

'Where's the sleigh gone?' Eddie asked Noah when they went into the barn.

'Back to where it came from,' Noah told him mysteriously.

'The flying reindeer have all gone too,' said Izzie, coming in with a wheelbarrow.

'They'll be back next year,' Noah told her. 'They always come back.' And he headed out to the fowl barn to feed the golden geese and singing chickens with two buckets of corn.

'It can't be, can it?' said Eddie, when Noah had gone.

Izzie smiled. 'Maybe,' she said. They were both thinking the same thing. It was almost Christmas Eve and Santa Claus needed a sleigh.

As they fed the woolly mammoths and unicorns their hay, Eddie and Izzie heard a roar followed by a screech and a howl. The tune was very familiar.

'They're singing "Rudolph the Red-nosed Reindeer",' Izzie said.

'Should be "Cornflake the Red-flamed Dragon",' Eddie told her and Izzie laughed.

The singing got louder and louder until they saw the bigfoot family coming through the trees.

'Snowball wants to play in the snow,' Toby said.

'Put some warm clothes on first,' said mum. She helped Toby to put on his winter boots and hat and scarf while the rest of them got ready.

As they were leaving the house Noah came out of the fowl barn where he'd been feeding

the singing chickens. The two younger
bigfoots excitedly pointed at his beard and
made chattering sounds. They beckoned to
their mum and dad as they headed over to
the old caretaker.

'Not too much touching . . . gently now!'
Noah said.

But Eddie could see his eyes were smiling
and he didn't mind too much as the bigfoots

tried to groom his *face fur*.

Meanwhile Snowball and Toby had been busily collecting up snow and rolling it into a ball.

They threw their snowball at Eddie and Eddie threw one back. Soon everyone was joining in the game, even Noah and Beth. Although the bigfoots were by far the best snowball makers. When they got tired of

throwing snowballs Beth came out with mugs of steaming hot chocolate to warm everyone up.

'This is the best Christmas ever,' Izzie said.

'Never had one like it,' said Dad.

'Every day's special at the Secret Animal Society sanctuary,' Mum said, as Toby and Snowball came running hand in hand and Cornflake flew over to join them.

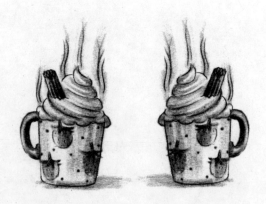